MW00974887

Glamorous Garbage

Barbara Johansen Newman

BOYDS MILLS PRESS
AN IMPRINT OF HIGHLIGHTS
Honesdale, Pennsylvania

Copyright © 2015 by Barbara Johansen Newman

All rights reserved

For information about permission to reproduce selections from this book,

please contact permissions@highlights.com

Boyds Mills Press, Inc.

An Imprint of Highlights

815 Church Street

Honesdale, Pennsylvania 18431

boydsmillspress.com

Printed in China

ISBN: 978-1-62091-626-1

Library of Congress Control Number: 2014943966

First edition

Designed by Tim Gillner

Production by Margaret Mosomillo

The text of this book is set in Galahad.

The display type is hand-lettered by Barbara Johansen Newman.

The illustrations are done in conventional and digital mixed media.

10 9 8 7 6 5 4 3 2 1

In memory of my grandmother, who could breathe new life into items old, outgrown, or discarded
—BJN

Bing-bong-bing the doorbell sang on Saturday.

"That must be Aunt Tessie and Joanie," Mom said.

Aunt Tessie is Mom's best sister. Joanie is my best cousin.
We are almost always together.

I jumped up.

"Opening the door?" Mom asked.

"Nope! Hiding in my room. Tell Joanie to come find me,"
I said. Then lickety-split, I ran upstairs.

My bedroom was a *teensy* bit full of stuff. But somehow I snuggled into the best hiding place. Then I didn't move a muscle—or even blink.

Joanie opened my door. "Bobbie?" she said.

I didn't answer.

She tiptoed between some robots and around my Pretty Poodle collection. "There's no space to walk in here," she said. "Did you fly into your room?"

That made me giggle. I jumped up and yelled . . .

"Surprise!"

Except I surprised myself. I bumped my head on the bookshelf, and it crashed to the floor.

Mom and Aunt Tessie came running. "Is everyone okay? What's all the racket?"

"I wanted to surprise Joanie, and my room went bonkers," I said.

"Bobbie, this room is *always* bonkers," Mom said. "You need to get rid of some of this stuff."

"No! I need all of it! It's my very favorite stuff in the world."

Mom shook her head. "This room is a problem, and the time has come to fix it. I'll give you two weeks to decide what stays and what goes. After that, *I* get to decide."

Mom put the shelf back up. Then she and Aunt Tessie went downstairs.

Joanie and I sat on my bed. "Your mom's right," she said. "This room *is* kind of a problem."

I looked around. "The problem is that it's a little-kid room," I said. "What I need is a glamorous big-kid room."

"What you need is a cleaned-up room," Joanie said. "It's no fun to play in here."

That night I had lots of room dreams. I woke up full
of ideas. I cut out pictures from magazines and made a
room poster. Then I showed it to my mom.

"This is what I want," I told her.
"Sorry, sweetie," Mom said. "We can't buy new things for
your room right now. But you can still clean it up."

"Getting a glamorous big-kid bedroom is not going to be easy," I told Joanie after school on Monday. "Just thinking about that makes me a grumpy head."

"Let's go to Sophie's Sweet Shoppe on the way home," she said. "Maybe some fireballs will cheer you up."

When we got there, Sophie was putting things by the door. I asked what they were for.

"For the trash," she said. "I have too much stuff. I'm running out of space."

All of a sudden, I had a great idea! "Can I have this stuff?"
I asked her.

"Be my guest," Sophie said. "You'll save me a trip to the dump."

Fireballs and free stuff! Joanie was right. Sophie's cheered me right up.

But Joanie wasn't so cheery. "What are you going to do with Sophie's trash?" she asked.

"This isn't trash. This is glamorous garbage!" I said. "Now I have a room plan."

"I think you need a plan to get rid of stuff, not collect it," Joanie said.

"You'll see," I told her.

When we got to my house, Mom met us at the door.
"Barbara Louise," she said. "What are you doing with that junk?"

"I have a room plan," I said.

"I'm not sure I like this plan," she said.

"You'll see," I told her.

"I hope so," Mom said. "But you have only eleven days left to
make it work."

After that, I found cool stuff everywhere.
I was a fearless explorer on garbage day.

I was the queen of yard sales.

My favorite place was the Swap Shed at the town dump, where I got great stuff for free!

Joanie helped, but she wasn't happy. "I can't believe you want this," she said. "It looks like something that isn't something anymore. Besides, you are running out of days to fix your room."

"I have plenty of time," I said. "And this stuff is too good to pass up."

One afternoon the next week, Joanie brought her Pretty Poodles over. Somehow, we cleared a place to play, and everything started out okay. Then all of a sudden, Joanie got upset.

"I can't find my purple poodle," she said. "I just had him! He was right here!"

We looked all over. We looked all under. We couldn't find him anywhere.

That's when Joanie started yelling. "There's no space to walk, and there's no space to play. This room isn't glamorous, it's a mess! And now it's made me lose my purple Pretty Poodle. No more stuff should come into this room until stuff goes out!"

You know what? Something *did* go out of my room that day. Angry Joanie.

It took a while, but I found Joanie's poodle in the only place we didn't look: behind my room poster. I looked at the poster, and I looked at my room. They were not alike at all! I was so busy collecting things that I forgot to use the things I collected.

Garden Party Room

That's when I knew it really *was* time to fix the problem of my room. I had a good plan in my head, but I didn't know where to begin. And my two weeks were almost up! I needed help!

I went and got my mom.

Then we put it back together again—
but in different ways. When we were
done, nothing looked the same as before!
   "Do you think Joanie will come over
and play now?" I asked my mother.
   "I have a feeling she will," Mom said.

On Saturday morning, the doorbell sang again. "That must be Aunt Tessie and Joanie," Mom said. "I'll answer the door."

"I'm going to hide," I said. "Tell Joanie to come find me in my room."

Lickety-split I ran upstairs. But my room was so neat and clean, all the old hiding places were gone. At the last minute, I found the perfect place.

A second later, Joanie opened my bedroom door.
"Bobbie?" she said.

I jumped out of my closet. "Surprise!" I yelled. And this time I didn't surprise myself. I surprised Joanie.

"Welcome to my glamorous, big-kid, made-with-help-from-my-mom-and-best-cousin room!" I said. I gave Joanie a hug and her purple Pretty Poodle. Then I gave her another surprise—something that I'd made into something again!

Joanie loved her present, and everybody loved my new room, even if it still was a *teensy* bit bonkers.

And, you know what else?